Henrietta

the great go-getter

Martine Murray

Macmillan Children's Books

ACKNOWLEDGEMENT

I would again like to acknowledge the very beautiful work of Verity Prideaux,
who made this book look as lovely as possible. Thanks also to Rosalind,
Sue and the original and best squidger, Sally Rippin.

First published in Australia in 2006 by Allen & Unwin
First published in the UK in 2007 by Macmillan Children's Books

This edition published 2008 by Macmillan Children's Books
a division of Macmillan Publishers Limited
20 New Wharf Road, London N1 9RR
Basingstoke and Oxford
www.panmacmillan.com

Associated companies throughout the world

ISBN 978-0-330-45192-5

Copyright © Martine Murray 2006

The right of Martine Murray to be identified as the
author and illustrator of this work has been asserted by her
in accordance with the Copyright, Designs and Patents Act 1988.

1 3 5 7 9 8 6 4 2

A CIP catalogue record for this book is available from
the British Library.

Cover and text design by Martine Murray and Verity Prideaux
Typeset by Verity Prideaux
Printed in China

Henrietta P. Hoppenbeek
would like to dedicate this book to
Rico and Mannie,
who accidentally landed on the
Wide Wide Long Cool Coast of the Long Socks
and made a LOVELY hullabaloo there.

The first book by Henrietta is
Henrietta
there's no one better

Henrietta the great go-getter

Hello everybody out there in the whirly old world

It's me, Henrietta.

I'm the future Queen of the
Wide Wide Long Cool Coast
of the Lost Socks, so you'd better
listen to me because otherwise
I might have your head chopped off
and mashed up like potato and fed to the crocodiles.

Not really.

Everyone knows crocodiles don't like mash.

They like
a cup of peppermint tea
and a strawberry
cupcake.

Not really.
Crocodiles only like to eat grown-ups
because they are fatter
and a bit grumpy sometimes.

And also, besides and on top of that, only very very
nasty wicked queens will chop off your head,
and actually I will be a very very perfectly nice
queen who doesn't dribble one bit.

Lordy Lordy, you should see my brother Albert.
He dribbles and dribbles, but he's only a baby
so he can't help it. He can't help doing rude
embarrassing things like

poo and **burps**
and **growling**.

It's lucky I'm not a baby
because I DO like to be dignified,

which means I poo in the loo
and I walk like a queen
and I eat ice-cream
without putting
it on my face.

I DO
like to be other things
as well.

For instance,
I'm very often
brave and **bold**,
and every now and then
I'm expOOperating
and expasperating
and ex**hill**perating.

8

If you don't know what that means ask your dad,
because dads like to tell you stuff they know about.

Don't be fooled, though.
They might know a lot about golf
or GERMAN PHILOSOPHERS or how
to fix a broken thing,
but dads don't know
about Riettas or
handstands,

and besides
and on top of that,
they've never been to the
Wide Wide Long Cool Coast
of the Lost Socks.

There's only one person in the whole
whirly old world who can tell you about that,
and that's

Henrietta the great go-getter.

So that's why you'd better listen.

There's
something going
on, and it isn't even
Christmas. I'll tell you what it
is. It's something in the house. It's a
D i l e m m a.
And if you don't know
what a Dilemma is,
don't worry because
I'll tell you now. A
Dilemma isn't quite a
first cousin of the
Dottypeejarma,
and it's only a very far
distant distant relation of the large dancing
Piggyleedrama, and, just in case you were
thinking it might be, a Dilemma isn't even a
creature at all, it's a PROBLEM. Like for
instance when you have a lost Rietta living in your
bedroom, which is exactly the problem I have.

Here's what a
Dottypeejarma
looks like.

Here's what
a large
dancing
Piggyleedrama
looks like.

13

You can see the Rietta is
sadder than the others,
and that's because it's lost.
A Rietta is a particular kind
of creature who helps you
clown around, and Riettas
are most definitely best
when they're happy. They
HOOT when they're happy.
I like hooting. I like to hear
it and I like to do it. But
what I like to say best of all
is Sheeza mageeza.
And when you have a
Dilemma, you don't just
say it as if you were saying,
'Oh dearie mearie, this is
a bit of a pickle.'
You say it with **oomph**
and you say it with
poomph like this...

What if you woke up next to a crocodile
rather than a Rietta?
Now that would be a BIG Dilemma.
Or what if your brother turned into a chocolate
ripple cake and you accidentally ate him because
you didn't hear him yelling out,
'It's me, Albert!'
That would also be a BIG BIG Dilemma.

mageeza

Or what if you found that you
yourself had shrunk to the size
of a peanut, and Albert sat on you
because he didn't hear you calling out,
'Hey watch it, fatty!'
That would be what I call a DISASTER.
Because this is what I'd look like if Albert sat on me.

And if I was FLAT, how would I get in the bath
and sail to other lands?
As far as I know, flat people can't sail
because they probably just flap around
like wet towels in the wind.
And sail we must!
We absolutely have to find the Rietta a home
because the sadder the Rietta becomes
the more its spots fade.
Just this morning I noticed the Rietta's spots
were as pale as a tissue and I felt very very concerned.

I rang up Olive Higgie and I said, 'You won't believe it, but I think we have an EMERGENCY DILEMMA here.'

'Oh dearie mearie,' said Olive Higgie, who is my best friend and who has been known to eat pickles. 'Poor poor Rietta. What will we do?'

'Oh Lordy Lordy,' said I, Henrietta the great go-getter. 'Well, we'll get in the bath and we'll go find the Pelican on the rock and we'll ask him where can we find a home for the Rietta, because that Pelican is a busybody who knows exactly precisely who is who and which is what and how a dot and why the plot and what the…

'Busybody? What's a busybody?' said Olive Higgie. 'A busybody,' said I, pretending not to notice that Olive Higgie had interrupted my poem, 'a busybody is someone who stands on a rock and watches all the goings on around him and tells anyone anything and forgets to do his exercises or write his own poems and often wears a red raincoat so that you don't mistake him for a mushroom or a lighthouse.' 'Oh,' said Olive Higgie. 'When do we leave?' And I said, Bathtime of course.'

Bathtime

Sheezamageezad, there's another Dilemma.
A Bathtime Dilemma. Guess who's in the bath?
Albert. Little fatty. He makes me laugh.
'Listen Albert, we've got serious business,' I say,
and he just smiles at me and I give him
a quick squidge, which is the kind of squeeze
you give someone you accidentally love.
'Okay little pumpkin,' I say, because that's what
Mum calls him, even though he doesn't look
one bit like a pumpkin because he's not orange.
'Okay little muffin,' I say, because that's also
what Mum calls him and I like muffins better
than pumpkins.

'Looks like you'll just have to come along
'cause we absolutely have to go and do some
serious explorification.'

Albert blows a raspberry.

'For the sake of the Rietta,' I add in a hushed
voice, just so Mum can't hear, because she
doesn't know about the Rietta.

Albert holds up the soap and says, 'fish?'

And I begin to wonder...

If Albert thinks the

soap is a fish,

and Mum thinks Albert is a pumpkin,

and Olive thinks pickles are yummy,

Pickles

then anything can be anything...

A bath 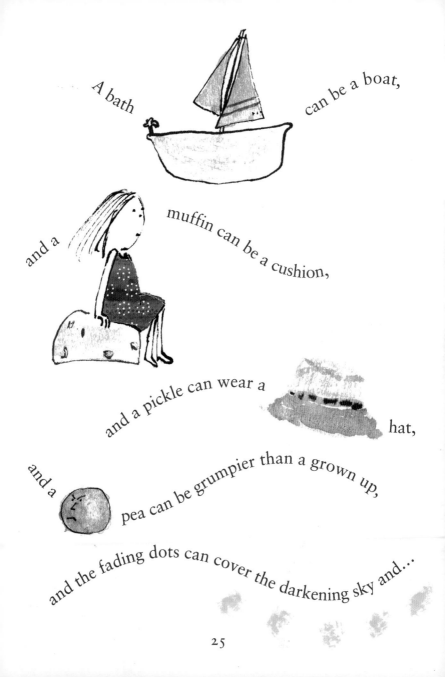 can be a boat,

and a muffin can be a cushion,

and a pickle can wear a hat,

and a pea can be grumpier than a grown up,

and the fading dots can cover the darkening sky and...

and the great

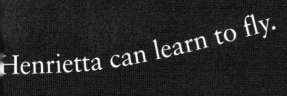

Henrietta can learn to fly.

Not really. Everyone knows
you have to eat lots of
brussels sprouts if you
want to learn to fly,
and I don't like
b r u s s e l s
sprouts.
N o t
o n e
bit.

So we'll have to sail after all.

I get in the bath with Albert
and the Rietta,

and we stop by to pick up Olive Higgie.
I whisper, 'This time we won't drop Albert
off in the Land of One Thousand Alberts
because we might just need him.'
Olive Higgie says, 'How could we possibly
need Albert? He can't even walk yet.'
'As an anchor, of course.'
Olive Higgie thinks a bit and then says,
'Okay, giddy-up,' because she's a bit excited
and has mistaken the bath for a horse.
Albert says, 'boat?' And the Rietta gives a little
hopeful HOOT and then we set sail
to find the Pelican.

The Pelican

The Pelican has his back to us,
so when we get close to his rock
I yell out and he jumps up and squawks,
'Good grief, good grief. Why must all little children
yell? It makes me feel jumpy and I only have
a small rock and if I jump I might land on the
wrong side of the rock and I try never never
to land on the wrong side of the rock.'
'Why?' I ask.
'Good grief. There you go. All little children ask
"Why?" Another most annoying habit. Especially
when there's no answer. Some things are just done
one way and not the other. Like when you eat toast
you put butter on one side and not the other. Now
how would you feel if some noisy yelling pelican
came along and asked you, "Why? Why do you put
your butter on that particular side of the toast and
not on the other particular side of the toast?"
Actually, come to think about it, why don't you put
butter on both sides? Hmmm?'

We all think about this for a minute. I have to admit it, that know-all squawker Pelican has a point. Before I can come up with an idea, which is what I usually do, he goes and squawks again,

'Good grief, what on earth are you doing with a **lost** Rietta on board?'

'It's losing its spots,' says Olive Higgie.

'Of course it is. All Riettas lose their spots when they're lost. Their spots don't like sad skin so they start to leave, and once a Rietta has lost its spots it isn't a Rietta any more.'

'Oh dearie mearie,' says Olive Higgie. The Rietta makes a sad little noise and tilts its head to the side, and I give it a reassuring rub on its back where it especially likes to be rubbed. Riettas are very very sensitive and Pelicans aren't one bit sensitive.

'What does a Rietta become once it loses its spots?'
I say.
'A pale shadow of its former self,' pronounces
the Pelican.
'What's that?' says Olive Higgie.
'It's a Moonbeam,' says the Pelican,
who holds out his wings for dramatic effect.
'Oh Lordy Lordy.'
'And further furthermore,' says the Pelican,
with an extra dramatic dip of his beak,
'you may wonder what indeed happens to the spots
when the Rietta loses them.'
'Do they become stars in the sky?' says Olive Higgie
hopefully, because she's a dreamy girl.

'I'm afraid not,' snorts the Pelican. 'The spots look for some happy skin. They look for frinkles and they look for squidges and for gurgles and for dribbles, for these are all signs of happiness, and the spots live off happiness.'

'What's a frinkle?' I ask.

The Pelican puffs himself up because if there's one thing a busybody pelican likes it's to know things that other people don't know.

'A frinkle is a fat wrinkle, of course.'

'Well, I'm not fat so those spots aren't going to land on me,' I say.

'Me neither,' says Olive Higgie, and then we both look at Albert who opens his mouth to laugh and

Sheezamageeza!

He's covered in spots. Pale blotchy spotty spots.
'Albert?' I gasp. 'Are you all right?'
Albert gurgles and dribbles
and makes a **grrrr** sound.
'Of course he's all right. He's happy as Larry.
That's why the spots are landing on him.
And if you don't get rid of those spots
he'll soon turn into a Rietta himself!'

Olive Higgie says, 'Who's Larry?' and I say,
'Don't worry about Larry. Oh Lordy Lordy, look,
now Albert really does look like a muffin. A smiling
gurgling sultana muffin.'

And the Rietta, well the Rietta is staring out to sea,
looking pale and thin as a sheet. I'm afraid to say it
but the Rietta is losing its frinkles.

'Oh Lordy Lordy, what shall we do?' I say.

'Poor poor Rietta. And poor poor poor Albert.'

'And poor poor spots,' says Olive Higgie,
because Olive Higgie is an arty girl who likes
spots and stripes and triangles and stars.

'I'll tell you what you'd better do,' declares the
Pelican, and his wings elbow the air out of his way
as he leans toward us. 'You better get to the
Wide Wide Long Cool Coast of the Lost Socks
very quick sticks. I've heard a rumour that there
just might be a small colony of Riettas living there!'

The Wide Wide Long Cool Coast of the Lost Socks

We sail as fast as a bath can sail directly towards the Wide Wide Long Cool Coast of the Lost Socks. We can see the lost socks lounging under the palm trees, sunbaking and relaxing and no doubt having some thoughts as well. Olive Higgie suddenly looks a bit afraid and she says, 'Henrietta, have you ever met a lost sock?'

'Not yet.'

'Well then how do we know the lost socks aren't nasty or cruel or very very bad?' I think about this for a minute, and since it's my job to be bold I say, 'When you're doing serious emergency explorification, then you have to be brave and hope for the best, but at the same time be prepared for the worst, which means we leave Albert on the shore, tied to the bath, so the bath won't float away. If the socks are nasty we can jump back in the bath and sail away on a cheerful breeze.'

Olive Higgie looks at Albert and then at me and then at the Rietta and then she nods her head and says, 'Okay, onwards brave soldiers,' because she's a bit afraid and has mistaken the Wide Wide Long Cool Coast for a battlefield.

So we tie Albert to the bath and leave him playing with a rubber duck. Then Olive Higgie and I and the Rietta creep up quietly towards the lost sock sunbaking area.

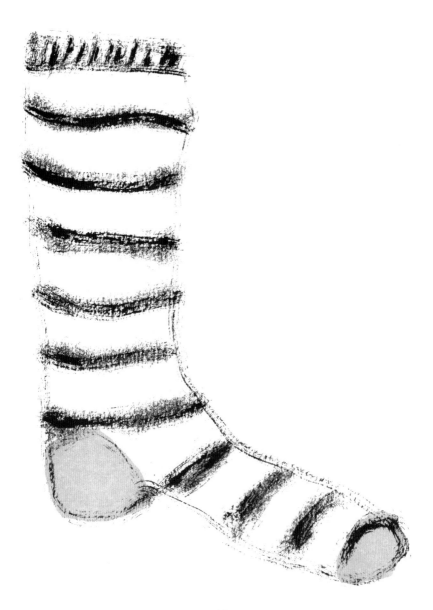

A long striped sock notices us first. He slowly wriggles up on his heel and says, 'Hey guys, are you lost?' 'No, no we're not lost, we're looking for the Rietta colony.' 'Dudes, if you're not lost then we can't let you on the island. Only lost socks, lost slobs and lost souls are allowed here. And that means no tourists, no superheroes and no astronauts.

'What's a dude?' whispers Olive Higgie to me,
and I whisper back that I suspect it might be
a person who comes from the town of Dudelings,
where they mainly say rude things, but I'm not
absolutely sure. Then I turn to the sock.

'We've got a Dilemma,' I declare, since future
queens are allowed to make declarations,
especially when the Rietta is getting paler by the
minute, which means that Albert is probably getting
fatter and starting to HOOT.

'A Dilemma?' says
Long Striped Sock.
'I never heard of a Dilemma.
Do we allow Dilemmas?'
'Only if they can sew,'
says a tattered looking
sock with holes.
Then I say in a loud
important voice,

'Excuse me but we're in a big hurry to find
this sad fading Rietta a home, because it's lost.'

LOST

screeches a smart black business sock.
'Why didn't you say that in the first place?'
And then all the socks pop up and hop over
and roll around the Rietta saying,
'Welcome to the club.'
And indeed the Rietta manages to HOOT,
because there's nothing a Rietta loves more
than being the centre of a hullabaloo.

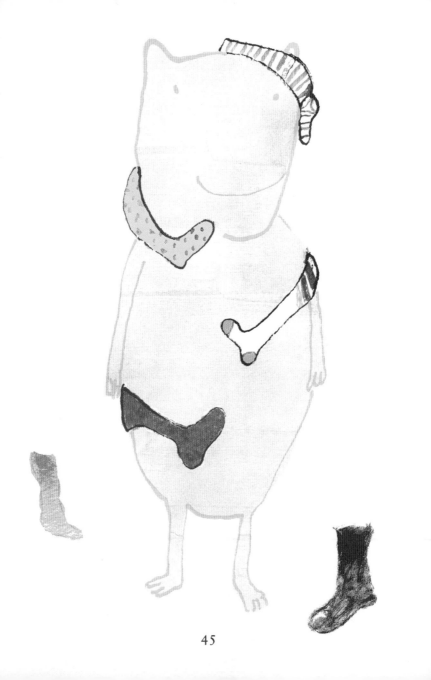

'He-hmmm,' I say, which is exactly the right thing to say when the attention is no longer on you and it absolutely should return to you. 'Excuse me, Lost Socks, but we have an EMERGENCY DILEMMA because we need to find a home for this Rietta V.Q.S. (which, in case you don't know, stands for Very Quick Sticks) or it will become a Moonbeam!'

Long Striped Sock says, 'Cool, a Moonbeam!'

Tattered Holey Sock says, 'Poor sod.'

Smart Black Business Sock says, 'Emergency Dilemmas are not allowed and Moonbeams are against the law, unless they are very smelly indeed.'

And just as I'm beginning to despair, a bouncy little tennis sock sidles up to me and whispers,

'I've got an idea, but you have to follow me.'

I have a consultation with Olive Higgie, since she is second mate.

'Would you trust a tennis sock?' I say.

And she has a quick think and says, 'If you would.'

So I have an even quicker think, and since I'm a very very quick thinker I don't even have time to hear my thoughts think before I say, 'Okay we'll follow.'

Because, let's face it, we don't have any choice but to trust a tennis sock.

Farewell O.H.

First of all we go over a big sand dune and then
we slide down the other side and come to a jungle.
There's a sign which says:

Beware
The Bungry
jungle

'Oh dearie mearie,' says Olive Higgie.
'Oh Lordy Lordy,' says I, because everyone knows
that there's nothing as hungry as a bungry.

Bungries eat anything,
you name it:
roast pork, roast unicorn,
roast great-aunt-susan,
even peas, beans and salad greens,
even brussels sprouts and pickles,
and probably your rubbish and your dirty washing,
and most probably your local dentist
and the prime minister,
though no one knows for sure.
But I know one thing for sure,
a bungry would love to eat
little girl explorers.

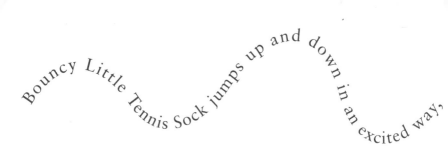

Bouncy Little Tennis Sock jumps up and down in an excited way,

which isn't very reassuring,
and Olive Higgie says,
'Perhaps I should go back and mind Albert?'
which is really an excellent idea.
I wish I'd thought of that myself,
but someone has to stay behind
and lead the explorification onwards.

'Farewell O.H.,' I say with a sniff.
O. H., in case you didn't notice,
is code name for Olive Higgie,
and code names
should always be used
when the explorification
has reached a possibly tragic
and important climax.
I watch O.H.
scuttle back V.Q.S.
to find Albert, and,
to tell you the truth,
I begin to feel a bit lonely.
But the Rietta rubs up
against me because
it knows I'm about to be
VERY BRAVE indeed.

'Ready?' says Tennis Sock, with an eager leap.
'Aren't you one bit afraid of being eaten?' I say,
since it's not every day you meet a fearless tennis
sock, so I'm curious.

'Bungries don't eat socks.'

'Oh I see. Well, lucky for you you're a sock
and not a person like me. What about
Riettas? Do bungries eat them?'
We both look at the Rietta,
who is now only a faint outline,
and the sock says, with a heartless giggle,
'They won't eat this one.
Nothing left to eat!'
I have a bit of an emergency ponder.
If bungries don't eat socks then I
might just disguise myself as a sock.
A blue spotty sock in fact,
since that is my very favourite kind.

I tell the sock my plan and it laughs and jumps
and says, 'Yes, what a joke. Good idea.'
Luckily there happens to be
an old leftover Christmas stocking
hanging from a Christmas tree,
and it's just exactly my size.

So I wriggle in and off we hop,
the tennis sock and I,
with the Rietta pattering along beside us.

The Bungry Jungle

Inside the sock,

in the deep deep depths
of the Bungry Jungle...

I can hear my heart going
thud thud thud very very loudly.
And I wonder if real socks have hearts,
and if a bungry just happened to hear
a heart inside a sock, would it be suspicious?
I try very hard to make my heart quiet,
but the harder I try
the louder it thumps
and the louder it thumps
the more scared I become
and the more scared I become
the louder it thumps
and the louder it thumps
the harder I have to try to stop it thumping,
which isn't working at all
because then,
quite suddenly...

there is a real live long hungry bungry nose
and it is sniff sniff sniffing,
and a suspicious bungry ear
listen listen listening
to my heart thud thud thudding,
and then, oh Lordy Lordy,
a bungry mouth open open opening and...

The bungry sneezes because the Rietta is tickling its nose and acting like a spooky ghost, and the bungry is scuttling back into the trees like a little scaredy cat.

PHEW.

The tennis sock
is laughing its heel off.
'What's so funny?' I ask
in the manner of a queen.
'I nearly got eaten.'
'Ha ha,' it says. 'Exactly!
What a hilarious joke I played.
See, everybody thinks
bungries will eat anything,
but there's a **Big** Secret
only lost socks know.'

'What's the secret?' I say,
because if there's one thing I love
it's discovering a **Big** Secret.
'Shhh,' says the sock.
Then it whispers,
'Do you know why
there's nothing
as hungry as a bungry?
Because bungries don't
eat anything except air.
Bungries don't really
eat people
or socks
or steaks
or anything.
They're AIR-ARIANS.'

Well I've heard of vegetarians, because that's
what my mum is, and my dad says he'd like to be
a roast lamb-arian, which means I might just as well
be a chocolate ripple cake-arian, but I've never
heard of an air-arian. I don't think I'd like
to be one of those.

Tennis Sock is still roaring with laughter.
'Yes, clouds for lunch, sunset for dinner and
blue skies for dessert. Ha ha, and you even dressed
up as a sock. Lucky you didn't dress up as a cloud.
Ha ha. Wait till I tell the others. Do excuse me
for making a joke at your expense, but it's so boring
down there on the shore. Too sunny and relaxing.
I do have to amuse myself somehow. Tennis socks
need a bit of a bounce.'

'Hmmph,' I say, which is exactly the thing to say
when a lost tennis sock has made you look
like a fool and you only half forgive them,
though there's a chance that if they are especially
nice to you, like if they read you a story or make
you laugh, then you will forgive them completely.

The Gel Site W.

There's no time for sulking because
the Rietta looks too tired to go much further.
So I get ready to keep going, but Tennis Sock
points us towards a dark tunnel.
'This is where I leave you, I'm afraid. You have to
pass through this tunnel. On the other side is the
Wide Wide Coast of the Woolly Wanderers.
But no sock has ever come out of that tunnel,
so no sock should go in.'
There's a sign in front of the tunnel:
Gel Site W. No body welcome.
'What does that mean?' I ask.
'No one knows,'
says Tennis Sock,
'but if you find out,
do tell me. Cheerio.'
The mischievous sock bounces away
and I think to myself that if a tennis
sock has a heart it is a small heart
that ticks like an alarm clock.

The Rietta and I
look at the tunnel.
'Well, Gel sounds like jelly,
so maybe it's nice and soft
and squishy in there,' I say
in a hopeful way, but the Rietta
doesn't believe me, and nor do I,
because, let's face it, this tunnel
isn't exactly looking like a fun palace.
It's dark and hollow and cold, and worst of all
there's a very stinky smell coming out.
The Rietta lies down and I realise it can't
go any further, which means that I'm the only one
left on the expedition. It's all up to me.
Henrietta the great go-getter.
I sigh loudly and pat the
Rietta and I say,
'Don't worry,
I'll save you.'
Then I close my eyes
and plunge bravely into the tunnel.

As soon as I enter, I hear a loud booming voice.

who's
there?

I can't see anyone but I smell someone, and,
I can tell you, whoever or whatever it is in there,
it really pongs.
'It's just me, Henrietta, and I'm only a small girl
who is passing through on my way to find
a Rietta colony. Sorry to bother you. I would have
knocked but there wasn't a knocker.'

'No body is welcome in here. And I don't like small girls,' says the angry voice.

'Oh dear, well, let me see. Do you like explorers?'

'I don't like no body and no body likes me and you better not come any closer.'

'Why not?' I say boldly, because everyone knows you shouldn't annoy someone who smells revolting and seems a lot bigger than you.

'Because I am a monster and I will chomp you with my rotting teeth and stomp on you with my huge feet and breathe on you with my foulest breath and dribble on you with my disgusting spit...'

'Dribble? Hmmph, that's nothing. I'm used to that. I bet you don't dribble as much as my brother Albert.'

'What? What did you say?' yells the monster, and then he steps forward out of the dark.

When I see him, can you imagine what I say?

sheezamageeza
And I say it with oomph
and I say it with poomph.
And then I say, in the manner of a queen,
'Excuse me but you forgot to get dressed
because he's only wearing his
underpants and two odd socks.

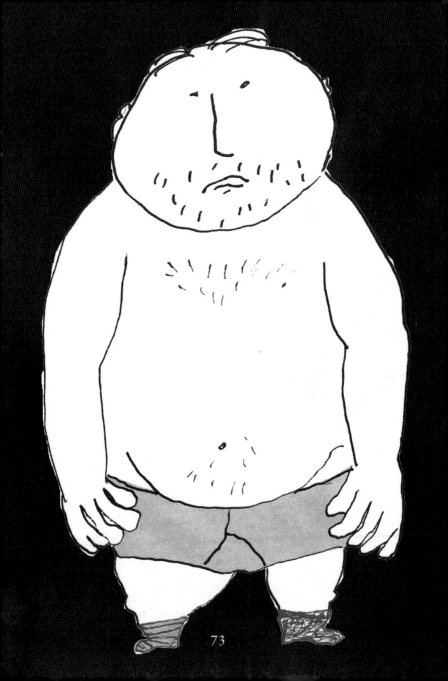

yellow stuff

sweaty

goobies

yucky stuff

hairs

mouldies

'Well
I wasn't
expecting
a visitor,'
he says.
And then
he roars,
'Now **you**
listen here,
young lady.
I've got
goobies
in my
nose holes
and mouldies
in my
toenails.
I've got
yucky stuff
between
my teeth

and
yellow stuff
in my ears.
I've got fluff
in my
belly button,
and hairs
on my
fatty bottom.
I've got
gooey gums
and pongy
breath and
grizzly plans
and sweaty
hands,
and no body,
I say
NO BODY,
can
beat that!'

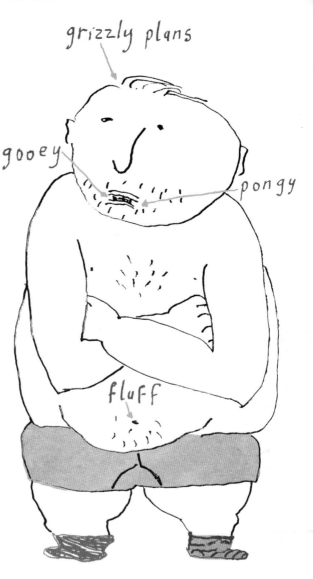

grizzly plans

gooey

pongy

fluff

'Albert can.'

'No he can't,' roars the monster.

'Do you poo your pants?'

'Of course I don't. That's DISGUSTING!'

'Well Albert does.'

'What?' he roars. 'You're making me very angry. This Albert is making me very angry. I'm afraid I'll have to take you for a prisoner and stuff you in my pillow with all the other lost socks. Unless, of course... well, there's only one way to save yourself now and that's to tell me what Gel Site W. stands for.'

Don't
you
know?'
'Of course
I know.
But
I've forgotten.
I live in
a dark tunnel.
I don't eat any
vegetables. I can't think
straight and I can't think curly,
I can't think at all. So if you can think
it for me, I'll let you go.'
'Fair enough,' I say, which is exactly what you
should say when a monster is making a deal with
you. I try to think. I try thinking straight and I try
thinking curly, but the only thought I can think
is that I might just be stuffed in a pillow and never
heard of again. Just when I'm about to give up,
I hear a familiar cry coming from far away.

'Oh dearie mearie.'

Boy am I happy to hear that. It's dear old O.H., and there she is on the other side of the tunnel, on the coast which is known as the Wide Wide Coast of the Woolly Wanderers. She's in the sea with Albert, bobbing up and down in the bathtub, and they're waving at me. And then O.H. is getting out of the bath and jumping, in a heroic fashion, onto the shore and hurrying V.Q.S. towards me. When she sees the monster, she stops and puts her hands on her hips and she says,

'Well, you must be the Greatest Ever Living Slob In The Entire World!'

And then the monster howls and roars and
stamps his ugly feet and moans
and I say, 'There there, she didn't mean it.'
And he says, 'Yes she did. She guessed it.
Gel Site W. That's what it stands for.

Greatest Ever Living Slob In The Entire World.

See, I'm not really a monster. I'm only a slob.'
'You're the Greatest Slob though. That's something,'
says O.H.
'What about Albert?' says the Greatest Slob.
'He poos his pants.'
At that moment O.H. and I both look at each other
because we remember that we've forgotten Albert
and the Rietta.
Olive Higgie says, 'Wait here, I'll get Albert.'
And I say, 'Wait here too, I'll get the Rietta.'
And the Greatest Slob starts to dribble.

Albert Saves the Day

When I return with the poor faded
Rietta, Olive Higgie is there with Albert
and something else as well.
'Look H.P.,' she says proudly.
'Look what Albert found.
When I got back to the bath
there was Albert, and he was
playing with a baby Rietta.'
Sure enough, there is a little spotty
grinning gurgling baby Rietta,
and when my big Rietta sees that baby
it begins to make a funny noise
like a pigeon. It takes the baby
in its paws and rocks it,
and a big tear rolls down its face
and it looks at me and HOOTS.
And I can't help it,
because I'm so happy
a big tear rolls
down my face.

Then I look at O.H. and Albert, because at times
like these you need your brother or your friend
or your sister or your dad to be by your side,
even for a moment, just in case all your big feelings
make you wobble or jump or explode.
But, Lordy Lordy, Albert is being picked up
by the Greatest Slob, and Albert isn't one bit scared
or disgusted. He just gives the Slob a big squidge,
because Albert loves everybody,
even if they are a slob.
And now the Greatest Slob is weeping.
'No one has ever cuddled me before.'

'Oh dear, that's very bad. Everyone needs
a cuddle and a squidge,' I say. 'But I'm afraid
you can't keep Albert because he's my baby brother
and I happen to like having him around,
and my mum and dad are quite mad about him too,
and we all like to get on the bed together and
have a bit of a roll and a giggle in the mornings.'
'What you need,' says O.H., 'is one of those
woolly wanderers out there to keep you company.
I happen to know that there is one in particular

who has just lost its friend.'
She points at one sitting out on the beach,
and the Greatest Slob puts Albert down
and walks over to the woolly wanderer.
O.H. is a very clever girl, and I'm feeling a little
jealous that she has come up with such
a fine idea which will possibly save us all.
She whispers to me, 'That woolly wanderer is
the one who has been looking after the baby Rietta,
so the poor thing is lonely.'

'Good thinking, O.H.,' I say,
because you have to
admit it when
someone else
on the team has
a good thought,
and then
I try to have
an equally
good thought,
but not
a better one,
just an equal one.
'Otherwise,' I say,
'I would
have to

take the woolly wanderer
home with me and
it would probably
eat all the ice-cream
and leave
dirty marks
on my sheets.'
'Good thinking
H.P.,' says O.H.
and then we
both feel
very satisfied
and very
EQUALLY
clever
together.

We watch the Greatest Slob and the lonely woolly wanderer say hello. The big Rietta and the baby Rietta begin to HOOT together, and you can see that the Rietta is becoming all fat and spotty again from the togetherness.

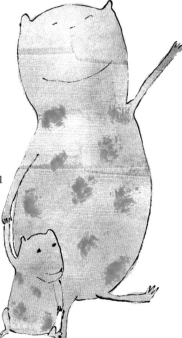

Then Albert starts to rub his eyes and that means we'd better jump in that bathtub and get him home, because if there's one thing that's almost as good as bathtime, it's bedtime, when Dad reads us a story about all the amazing things that can happen…

I give the Rietta a big squidge,
and the Rietta gives me a big squidge,
and even though it won't be living
in my bedroom, I know that whenever
I need to make a hullabaloo and have a
HOOT, I can just remember the Rietta
and know that it's making a hullabaloo
and having a HOOT too. And in some
way we will always be together.